Meant to Be

By Kanishka Nahar

Cyscoprime Publishers

Parijat Extension, Bilaspur, Chhattisgarh 495001
First Published By Cyscoprime Publishers 2020
Copyright © Kanishka Nahar 2020
All Rights Reserved.
ISBN: 978-93-90197-19-4
MRP: Rs.199/-

About The Book

Kaamya is an ambitious girl who has her eyes set on her goals.

She does not think she can fall in love because she is scared of heartbreak but as she starts meeting Kabir her fear soon converts into love and she falls in love with him.

After they share some breathtaking times together Kaamya and Kabir mutually end their relationship due to their goals.

Five years later Kaamya and Kabir meet at their favourite coffee shop and fall in love again.

Kaamya then says, "What is meant for me will find me."

About the Author

Kanishka Nahar is a student who loves writing! For her writing is a way to express her thoughts and emotions.

She wanted to take her love for writing a step further so she decided to utilize her time in this period of lockdown by writing a book.

A book which comes straight from her heart and by which she hopes to touch many hearts too.

Acknowledgement

Firstly I have to thank my mom, Poonam Nahar who has read all my drafts, stayed up in the night with me and been so supportive.

My dad, Siddharth Nahar for always inspiring me and telling me that everything is possible.

My grand mother, Sarla Nahar for being so motivating and supportive, and always giving me the best advice.

My grand father, Raikumar Nahar for setting a great example.

My maternal grandmother, Kanta Bumb, for always telling me to follow my heart

I would also like to thank my English teacher Rajlakshmi Vinod, who has made me capable.

The director of my school, Monica teacher, who has been like a mother to me and supported me always.

My friends,

Murtaza pipariyawala, who has always supported me and helped me get my spirits high when I had lost hope.

Shourya mehta, for always believing in me.

Zyra Irani for reading the books draft in a day so that I could be confident.

Jainaa Rathod, for always helping me out with struggles and believing in me more than myself.

Sidhant dhere, for being a Bollywood freak like me and giving me crazy ideas

Kimaya harnik, for writing so well and inspiring me always.

Cyscoprime publishers for giving me this amazing opportunity and Vikram Thakur for always being available.

Contents

Chapter 1

20th April 2019

At the airport.

Some people say that goodbyes said at the airport are usually the toughest ones but airports are actually places where not only planes but even dreams take off and fly

Kaamya Sinha, an ambitious, strong-willed girl from Pune was at the airport with her boy best friend Sanket. Sanket was good looking and smart, but lived in Bombay. Kamya and Sanket had been friends for five years and their friendship had been bulletproof ever since. They always had each other's back and were proud of each other during times of success. Kaamya often said every girl needs a boy best friend, well I guess that's true.

Kaamya had an amazing social life with supportive and fun friends who always needed her advice. She called herself their therapist and as it is said single people usually give couples the best advice, Kaamya too gave great advice. She hadn't fallen in love yet because she was waiting for that one guy who would truly love her and when she sees him her eyes will light up. She said, "I never chase anything, what is mine will come to me anyway."

As Kaamya and Sanket hugged each other a tear fell from her face she would never accept it but she would miss Sanket a lot. She quickly wiped her tears before Sanket could see them and make fun of her and then he left.

She waited for him as he turned around and waved and saluted, it was one of their rituals. Then she turned around and started walking towards the car reminiscing all the fun, gossip, pranks, and deep conversations that they had had over the past few days. She felt blessed to have him in her life.

She drove back home listening to their favourite song. Just as she ran up the stairs of her house feeling weirdly sad she saw her mom Ritu and dad Shyam trying to dance to some 90's Bollywood song with her younger sister Aahna trying to choreograph it and her grandparents Rishi and Madhuri were in charge of the music and she cracked up, then she realized that with her entertaining family she could never be sad for too long. They would always unintentionally make her laugh.

Soon it was movie night and Kaamya fell asleep watching "Kuch Kuch Hota Hai." That's when Kaamya's parents started discussing her and how proud they were! Their daughter was an all-rounder she was good at sports, singing, dancing, painting, debating, and studies. She had way too many potential careers!

22nd April 2019

The next morning Kaamya woke up at 4 am and started crying because she had dreamt of falling in love and having her heartbroken. Yes, that is how scared she was of having her heartbroken.

When she opened her window she saw that it was raining, the sky was crying with her. The clouds were

Grey, it was dark and the thunder gave Kaamya chills, but she loved the rain it made her feel alive. So she went out and danced in the rain. It made her heart happy.

She was a girl who loved life, she found happiness in the smallest of things like the raindrops on leaves or the wind blowing through her hair.

Then Kaamya got dressed and left for college.

Oberoi international was her dream school and she had two best friends over there Jenny and Mehul. She was friends with a lot of people but she opened up to very few.

Three of them had decided to bunk college that day and so they left for the mall. On the way, they were screaming at strangers and waving at them randomly. They reached phoenix and like every girl Kaamya loved shopping but she liked having fun even more so you won't believe what happened next. Kaamya chose a dress, went inside the changing room, changed into the dress, stole the dress, and left the store with her friends.

After they rushed out of the mall Mehul asked

"Kaamya you have the money to afford all this then why did we just shoplift?"

She replied, "it's never about the money it's about the thrill, the adventure that makes you feel alive."

None of her friends would understand her obsession with the word "alive".

But to Kaamya alive was the meaning of life. She wanted to live every moment like it was her last.

24th April 2019

It was time for Kaamya's results to come out. Kaamya knew she hadn't done very well because a day before her exams her great grandfather who she really loved passed away! It was hard for her, instead of studying all she did was cry. The tears wouldn't stop and her eyes were burning but she still expected things from herself.

When she looked at the result board all she could see was her failure. For the first time in her life, she felt like she had disappointed her parents and even though they told her that it was ok and that they understood her grades were low due to the circumstances during her exams, Kaamya couldn't look at herself, she felt ashamed.

She called Jenny and said, "Jenny I feel like I have failed, at life, like everyone is just looking down at me."

And that is when Jenny replied, "It's ok to feel weak sometimes and not be your best, everyone has their own share of success and failure if you don't fail you will never feel proud of being a success."

That changed Kaamya's outlook on life, she realized that being ambitious is great but what was more important was having acceptance, she needed to accept and love every version of herself, the success and the failure, the best and the worst one. As it is said, "before you expect someone else to love you, learn to love yourself." From that day Kaamya became a huge believer of self-love. She started loving herself truly and unconditionally.

25th April 2019

Kaamya was at her brother Raj's house. Raj and Kaamya had been extremely close since they were born. They practically raised each other and their bond was something anyone would want with their cousin. Kaamya dragged Raj to the mall, Raj made Kaamya play videogames, they went for trips and sneaked out of the house together, they spoke about everything they were best friends!

Kaamya and Raj were playing basketball and then Kaamya went to Jenny's house. Jenny was going to make Kaamya meet another friend of hers; this wasn't the first time Jenny was going to introduce her friends to Kaamya so Kaamya wasn't really bothered.

Soon Jenny got a call from her friend asking her where she was so Kaamya and Jenny went to get Jenny's friend Kabir.

A lean, fit guy with shades on and great shoes walked out of the car. He looked good and he was extremely confident. Moreover, he loved himself, actually not only did he love himself but he was self-obsessed! There was something about him that made Kaamya's heartbeat rise. She couldn't stop looking at him. He had this strong, charismatic personality. That was Kabir, everyone's favourite; he had a charm that would make anyone go crazy.

Then all of them played some fun sports.

Kaamya and Kabir's chemistry was undeniable! The look in their eyes showed the intensity in their hearts, but life went on and Kaamya forgot about Kabir

27th April 2019

It was a sunny morning and Kaamya looked forward to an eventful day.

First, she was going to meet Jenny and Kabir at Cafe coffee day and then she had a group study at Jenny's house. She loved the idea of studying together and making boring things fun.

She reached Cafe coffee day at 10 and met Kabir, Jenny was late as usual. Kabir ordered a java chip for Kaamya and him. He was a true gentleman! They spoke about things and turns out they were similar yet different but there was a click, a connection and then Jenny came. But they both knew it was the beginning of something, something special.

Then Kaamya went to Jenny's house and they started talking, gossiping and dancing around, both of them forgot that they had to study, but isn't that what friends do? They make you forget about all your problems and what bigger problems than studies right?

Anyway, then Kaamya went home and chilled with her neighbours, Reshma aunty who was practically her mother, Riya and Akash, they were Kaamya's family after her family. She loved them and would go to the ends of the world to make sure they were fine!

Kaamya and Riya ganged up and started teasing Akash. Kaamya got his legs, Riya held his hands and they lifted him and started swaying him from left to right. After that Kaamya had dinner at Reshma aunty's house because Reshma aunty had made her favourite pizza and they sat and spoke about food all night. Yes, indeed Kaamya was a foodie.

They were times like these that Kaamya loved her life the most! She felt grateful.

28Th April 2019

The last few days had been amazing for Kaamya but then she had a fight with Sanket. Kaamya had started a writing page where she wrote about her beliefs, majorly about self-love and feminism. For those of you who don't know feminism is the belief that men and women should have equal rights and opportunities.

Sanket thought that Kaamya was going against men so he said "I don't understand what your problem is with us men!"

Kaamya replied by saying "I don't have a problem with men, I have a problem with all those people who think men are superior to women."

Due to this, they started fighting and when Kaamya fought with Sanket she felt like her entire world had come crashing down. She tried to be very tough but her best friend was her weakness.

Sanket could not see Kaamya sad and he hated it when they fought so he decided to surprise her to compensate for their recent fallouts.

When Kaamya went home she saw a box at the door with her name on it, she opened the box and saw that it had her favourite cupcake with a note on it.

The note said "hey best friend! I'm sorry I said all those things to you I didn't mean it at all, now stop with all your drama. Love Sanket."

Kaamya sent him a message saying "finally someone knocked some sense into you! I knew you couldn't be pissed at me for too long and I am leaving my drama only for you."

All of Kaamya's friends were jealous of her because they had everything that Kaamya had except one thing, that was, Sanket. Everybody thought that Kaamya and Sanket were dating but both of them knew that their friendship was too pure to ruin with such stupid tags. A lot of times tags ruin the most beautiful relationships.

Chapter 2

1st May 2019

Kaamya and Raj had gone for a vacation and when they came back they saw that Raj's house was a complete mess, everything was shattered, the mirrors were broken and the safe was empty! Kaamya and Raj got worried when they enquired and asked their neighbours they said that a theft had taken place and when they tried to contact Raj his phone was switched off, that was because Raj had lost his phone during the trip. Raj and Kaamya decided that they had to get to the bottom of this.

Both of them called their most trusted friends Kaamya called Riya and Jenny and Raj called Kabir and Naksh. While they were looking at the house they saw a paper. Naksh was a topper and his brain would help them find who the thief was.

When Kaamya lifted the paper she saw that the page had Raj's daily schedule from the time he woke up to the time he came back home written on it.

That is when they realized that the thief didn't just want money but he also wanted to kidnap Raj, but they weren't able to kidnap him because he wasn't at home as Kaamya and raj had left the house early in the morning. They were all extremely scared and didn't want to leave Raj alone even for a minute but Raj protested and said that he would be fine, he was being extremely stubborn, and even though none of them were convinced they left his house as they had other things to do.

6th May 2019

The last few days had been extremely stressful and they hadn't let Raj go out of their sight but now everyone almost forgot the incident because Raj had been safe for almost a week now. He was living his life very normally and Riya and Raj had actually started meeting a lot, Raj really liked Riya. They both looked good together and everyone was teasing them. During this time even Raj and Kabir had become close friends and they also found out that they had met before.

Kaamya said "now that both of you have each other you will forget us"

Kabir said "find me also someone." After saying that Kabir looked at Kaamya.

Jenny said "Kaamya you truly are a matchmaker!" and everyone started laughing.

Then all of them decided to go to German Bakery in Koregaon park and

Ate a lot of food.

Then Kaamya and Raj left for home. That is when Kaamya confessed to raj that she did have feelings for Kabir, not intense ones but they were enough to give her butterflies. Even the thought of falling in love gave Kaamya chills! But deep down She was hoping that Kabir liked her too

At the same time, Kabir also confessed to Jenny saying that he liked Kaamya a lot! Jenny was so happy. She knew both of them would make the perfect couple.

That night Kabir took the first step and called Kaamya she was so nervous to take the call because she had never felt this way! She texted Sanket and Sanket almost fell off his bed when he heard that Kaamya liked someone, he even texted Kaamya saying "I feel really bad for Kabir! He doesn't know what he's getting himself into!"

Kaamya and Kabir spoke for a while and made plans to meet the next day.

It was the first time in Kaamya's life that she was wondering what she should wear, usually she wouldn't be bothered but this time she wanted to look perfect.

She chose her outfit as soon as she hung up on Kabir and couldn't wait for the next day to start!

7th May 2019

Kaamya woke up with a smile on her face. She couldn't wait to meet Kabir! She called Raj to inform him and Raj told her that he would also be meeting Riya today.

Kaamya got dressed and left her house to meet Kabir and Raj called Kaamya and told her that it would be better if four of them could meet so that it wouldn't be awkward and Kaamya thought that was a good idea, but when Kaamya and Kabir reached Ritz Carlton, Raj and Riya were not there.

Kaamya thought Raj was late as usual and she told Kabir that he would turn up in a while but they waited and no one came then Kaamya called Raj but his phone was switched off and when she called Riya her phone was switched off too.

Kaamya was hoping this was a coincidence but Kabir told her that waiting even a second more would be foolishness so Kaamya called Jenny and Kabir called Naksh.

Jenny and Naksh were there within no time, it turns out both of them also really liked each other and once they arrived Kabir told them that Kaamya thought that Raj and Riya's absence was connected to the theft a week back.

The second they heard that they rushed to Raj's house and thankfully Kaamya had a spare key!

They opened the door and tried to find the sheet the kidnapper had left the other day hoping that it would at least give them an idea. They split themselves into groups of two Kabir and Kaamya were one group and Naksh and Jenny were the other. Jenny and Naksh were going to try to track Raj and Riya's phone, while Kabir and Kaamya were going to try to find the sheet.

Without wasting any time the four of them got to work.

Soon Kaamya found the sheet and Kabir and Kaamya were now trying to find a hint but suddenly the lights went off so Kaamya went and got a candle while Kabir used the torch in his phone.

Kaamya was just walking with the sheet trying to figure it out but due to the bad light, she couldn't see anything so she put the sheet above the candle and suddenly she saw a map!

A map that leads to the outskirts of Pune. To be precise a storage room. Kaamya called Kabir and both of them thought that this was their only lead to find Riya and Raj.

As they were about to leave for that place Jenny and Naksh came running to the room and Jenny said, "we tracked them they are in the outskirts of Pune!"

Both the groups exchanged the information that they had gathered and rechecked to make sure it was the same location. Indeed it was!

All of them ran out of the house. Kabir got the car and they left for the location. Kabir drove as fast as he could and once they reached the place they tried looking for Riya and Raj but they weren't there. Just when the two pairs were about to give up Naksh saw a handle on the floor of the basement so Naksh tried to open it and turns out it was a door! He opened the doof and one by one they went inside! The minute Kaamya jumped in she saw Raj and Riya!

She had never been so happy to see her brother again but they were tied. So Kaamya and Jenny tried to distract the kidnappers and untie the ropes while the boys called the police. Soon the ropes were untied but the girls were caught by the kidnappers.

Kabir and Naksh's heart started pounding just when they were about to find the love of their life someone was taking them away from them! They begged and pleaded the kidnappers to let go of Kaamya and Jenny while they were trying to get close to them, suddenly the police siren was heard. Everyone sighed in relief and the kidnappers were shocked they left Kaamya and Jenny and tried to run but the police caught them.

As for Kaamya and Jenny the second the kidnapper let go of them they ran into Kabir and Nakshs arms! Both of them had never felt so happy before! Not only had they saved Raj and Riya but they had also found love.

On their way back home everyone was in a bad mood, they were thinking what would have happened if they hadn't found Raj and Riya. So that's why Raj tried to lighten everyone's mood up.

He said "even if the kidnapper hadn't left Kaamya and Jenny after few days he would pay us to take them back! These girls are nuts" everybody laughed.

Kaamya replied by saying "today these nuts have only saved you. Otherwise, god knows where you would be!" and from here onwards everybody started cracking jokes.

On the way, Kabir saw a waterfall and stopped the car! Everybody started climbing to jump from the top.

The rocks were very slippery and that's why Kaamya's leg slipped and she was holding the rock by her hand. She tried to hold on and shouted Kabir's name. Kabir came and tried to pull Kaamya up!

Raj, Kabir, and Naksh had formed a chain and were holding each other and finally, they pulled Kaamya up!

After that incident, Kaamya was not in the state to have fun. So Kabir took her down to the car and sat with her. That was the first time Kaamya and Kabir had a deep conversation. They spoke about their goals, parents and their failures!

Kabir asked Kaamya "what do you fear most?"

Kaamya replied, "I fear getting my heartbroken."

Kabir said "Kaamya maybe if you give your heart to someone instead of breaking it he would give you his own heart! You need to take a risk."

That's when Kaamya started trusting Kabir

Kabir continued "I promise that if you give me your heart I will never break it."

Kaamya said, "and I promise if you ever leave I will wait for you because if we are meant to be we will be."

Kabir smiled and said, "there is no if, WE ARE MEANT TO BE."

That one sentence made Kaamya blush and then everybody came back from the waterfall and they drove back home.

Kabir dropped everyone off and then went for a drive with Kaamya and they spoke as nothing had happened.

Finally, things would go back to normal. Kaamya couldn't wait for her next meet up with Kabir!

Chapter 3

9th May 2019

That day and for the next few days all Kaamya thought about was Kabir.

That boy had stolen her heart and she was happy with it but he hadn't asked her to be his girlfriend yet.

They were going to meet at 10. So Kaamya left her house and she reached Café Coffee Day, now Kabir knew Kaamya's java chip without whipped cream order by heart so he was waiting for her with it, Kaamya smiled at that. These little things meant a lot to her.

Then she suggested that they should walk so they walked through the lanes of that beautiful place. Kaamya had never been so happy in her life. They spoke about everything and now they even had inside jokes. Kaamya was going to spend the entire day with Kabir.

Then they went to a restaurant where they ate some amazing food and both of them had this one interesting conversation

Kaamya asked, "do you believe in self-love?"

Kabir replied "I think more than loving yourself believing in yourself is important because if you believe in yourself then you can achieve whatever you want. If you believe in yourself then you can inspire others too but just by loving yourself you can't love others"

Kaamya asked with curiosity in her eyes "do you love yourself?"

Kabir answered, "I do love myself but what I love a little more is a girl with a beautiful soul."

Kaamya smiled and said "oh! Who's that unlucky girl?"

She loved teasing Kabir as he would always get annoyed then both of them went back to Café Coffee Day and something amazing happened next.

Kaamya and Kabir were standing on top of the tables and dancing, they didn't care about the people who were looking at them but what mattered the most to them was having a good time.

Then they sat down and started judging and making faces at strangers. They were also trying to find hot girls and guys for each other and they were discussing the kind of people they want, it was then that both of them realized that they were exactly what the other one needed.

Kaamya was very imaginative and Kabir was a realist he would always ground Kaamya's thoughts. Kaamya was like the water she would go with the flow and Kabir was like her bridge he would stop her when necessary. Kaamya loved fairy tales she hoped that her life would be like a movie and Kabir was the man who told her that if she wanted her life to be like a movie she had to work for it. Kabir gave Kaamya stability and Kaamya gave Kabir a thrill and a reason to wake up every~day,

Then they started playing charades and the way their minds were connected was mind-blowing. They were practically reading each other's minds! Both of them didn't want this day to end but of course, they had to return to their respective lives and respective homes without each other. That day Kaamya was so happy that she was literally speaking to cab drivers, putting her head out of the window and singing songs she didn't even like.

When Kaamya and Kabir were together they didn't see anyone or anything else they just enjoyed each-others company and they even had fun just looking at each other

Kaamya texted Raj saying that she had never been happier in her life and that is when Raj told her that he was in a relationship with Riya! Kaamya was so happy she felt like she was on cloud nine!

What better news than her brother dating one of her closest friends.

She was so happy for Raj that she wanted to celebrate so instead of going to her house she went to Rajs house instead and both of them spoke about Kabir and Riya all night. That night was the first time Raj heard Kaamya be so serious about a boy otherwise usually the only thing she was serious about was her future. Raj wanted to make sure that even Kabir was serious about Kaamya.

10th May 2019

So the next day Raj met Kabir and asked him "what do you think about my sister?"

He replied saying "I think your sister is the world's most beautiful girl and her soul is extremely pure. She makes me feel alive and I wake up every day just to see her smile."

Raj was convinced that Kabir really liked Kaamya because instead of calling her hot he called her beautiful and instead of only talking about her looks he spoke about her soul.

After a while, He was going to meet Kaamya. Kaamya texted him saying she would be late because she had some news for him.

He kept hoping it would be good news!

When both of them met Kaamya didn't say a word.

After about 10 minutes she finally broke the silence and said "Kabir I was late because my dad called me to his office, when I reached there he told me that I have to go to Rajasthan to take care of my aunt and I don't really have a choice."

Kabir asked "so when are you leaving?"

Kaamya replied, "today night, my plane flies at 9 pm."

Kabir was speechless he just said, "oh ok take care of your aunt."

Kaamya said, "Kabir take care of yourself."

As she was about to leave he said, "Kaamya wait!"

She stopped and he said, "I'll miss you Kaamya."

After saying that he gave her a tight hug and that hug made Kaamya feel happy even in times of stress.

She then left and on her way to the airport and texted Kabir, "will you wait for me?"

He replied within seconds "I will, always, not only for months but even for years."

As soon as she read that she knew that he was the one for her, the only one.

Kabir felt lost without Kaamya even though he always knew what was good for him he felt like a huge part of his life was missing!

He missed her eyes, her smile, the way she teased him, her love for adventure and thrill, but mostly he loved the way she would make him forget everything and just make him smile.

Kaamya on the other hand was too busy taking care of her aunt.

Her aunt was now her responsibility and she wanted to make sure that she acted like a responsible adult.

Two months passed, Kaamya and Kabir spoke on text or call every day but the distance had put a pause to the love story. Kabir didn't want to start a relationship virtually so both of them decided to put a pause to things for a bit, but continued to keep their promises. At least Kaamya hoped they were.

3 months later

13th August 2019

Months had passed by very quickly and Kaamya couldn't wait to finally go home. But sadly her aunt was very sick and couldn't survive. But Kaamya had come to terms with the reality of life, and what bigger reality than death? Death is the most painful truth but it is also uncontrollable and inevitable. It's like a horrible surprise.

One day all of us have to die but I wish that death gave us a time period so that we could properly say goodbye

Kaamya kept thinking about her aunt on her way back home and how she became very close to her aunt because of spending so much time together.

The minute Kaamya stepped out of the airport, she saw Kabir! Her eyes lit up, she ran and gave him a hug but he didn't hug her back! With Kabir she felt free and she felt like she could make any pain go away

But then Kaamya saw a girl step out from Kabir's car, Kaamya stopped hugging Kabir and looked at the girl, in all of the family pictures that Kabir had shown her she hadn't seen this girl in any of them which meant she wasn't family but then she wondered "why would he bring a friend to the airport?"

That is when Kabir said "Kaamya I didn't want you to find out from anybody else but I couldn't keep my promise and even you know the distance is not my thing so this is my girlfriend Lara."

Kaamya couldn't believe it, the one thing that she was so scared of had just happened to her, heartbreak.

Kabir had shattered Kaamya's heart into pieces within seconds.

As she was about to cry Kabir started laughing and said

"Haha Kaamya stop taking everything so seriously this is my cousin Lara from abroad, she just came and I couldn't leave her home alone."

Kabir thought it was funny and that Kaamya needed to lighten up! But Kaamya was furious she didn't understand why Kabir would ever prank her like that! Especially when she had just suffered from a great loss! She had just lost her aunt.

Instead of being there for her, Kabir was joking around like nothing had happened so Kaamya told Kabir that she needed someone who was serious about her.

Kaamya then told Kabir "my family and I are already suffering so it would be better for us if people who don't take us seriously stay away from us."

Kabir couldn't believe it he tried to make her stay but when Kaamya made up her mind she wouldn't listen to anyone.

She just left.

Maybe Kaamya did overreact but her aunt who she dearly loved had just died so if that was Kabir's way of trying to comfort Kaamya by pranking her with the one thing she feared the most, Kabir was definitely being insensitive.

Lara said, "I told you it wouldn't make her happy but when do you listen to me."

Kabir had to do something he couldn't lose Kaamya over a stupid prank.

So the next day Kabir spoke to Lara and they planned a surprise for Kaamya.

They even involved Raj, Mehul, and Jenny in the surprise because Kaamya wouldn't even reply to Kabir's texts or answer his calls.

Raj, Mehul and Jenny were happy to help because they just wanted to see Kaamya happy and they knew that Kabir would make her happy!

Kabir also wanted to make sure that everything was perfect so he was super stressed.

14th August 2019

Kaamya didn't want to wake up, she felt miserable, first she lost her aunt and now Kabir. Then she tried spending time with her family it was so weird because with them time flew it was already 6 pm.

She spent the next few hours thinking about her life and how it had changed for the better and the worse, but they say it's a part of adulting. Kaamya thought to herself

"I don't want to become an adult! Once you're an adult each and every action that you take has harsh consequences!" as you all know by now Kaamya loved taking risks but she never had to face the consequences but once she grew up she realized that everything she did now had a repercussion.

She was in deep thought when suddenly Raj called her and said "Kaamya I'm in trouble! Please help me out!"

Kaamya asked "what's wrong Raj?

He said "I can't tell you on the phone meet me in my house in 30 minutes! Please don't cancel last minute this is really important. It's about Riya and I and no one else will understand. Please meet me all I have is you.

Kaamya was mentally exhausted and looked like a mess as she had cried all night, even her eyes were swollen so she didn't know whether she would go or not.

Chapter 4

Kaamya thought about it and decided that she would go to her brother's house because he had always been there for her, but suddenly Kaamya got a text from Raj it said "meet here as soon as possible." With a location attached to it. Kaamya was worried about Raj so she went to the location and as she reached there got really scared because it was bare land with no people at all! She was hoping no incident had taken place again.

Then suddenly she saw Raj enter in a formal suit and he gave a chit to Kaamya, the chit said

"Hey, beautiful! I want you to know that you are the most amazing person I have ever met and my life feels incomplete without you, you have become such a big part of my life in such a short time. Thank you for being so adventurous and making me do things I didn't think I would do like to dance on tables in Café Coffee Day! You have a gorgeous smile so keep smiling.

Kabir."

Kaamya couldn't help but blush! She was so happy that she had someone who actually took an effort to make her smile.

Then suddenly Mehul popped up with Kaamya's favourite chocolate.

After that Jenny came with a bouquet of red roses, Kaamya loved red roses and she loved how Kabir had involved her family and friends

Then finally Lara came with a blanket and some popcorn and said "I'm sorry about the prank, can we please start over again?"

And Kaamya said yes within seconds.

Then she saw a projector, a car and Kabir standing on top of the car with a sorry sign and he came to her and told her to look at the ticket and when she saw the ticket it was an old Bollywood movie which was not available anywhere and one-day Kaamya had just told

Kabir about the movie, she couldn't believe he paid attention to all those small useless things that she said.

Then they got in the sports car, the roof opened and they watched the movie and after that they spent sometimes just looking at the stars.

Kaamya loved the night and the stars because even in so much darkness the stars would still shine and the moon would guide her through the dark.

When the city was asleep Kaamya and Kabir's love story was ALIVE.

Then Kabir took her to this momo shop which was open at that hour and ordered the world's best momos.

The manager of the place knew Kabir and asked "is she someone special? You always come here alone you've never bought a friend with you"

Then Kabir explained "yes. She is someone special, in fact the only special person in my life."

Kaamya was extremely happy her life had become better than any movie and the person who made life worth living actually thought she was special.

Just when Kaamya thought that the night couldn't get any better Kabir said

"Kaamya I know you're scared of heartbreak and that is why today I want to promise you that I will never break your heart! You have made me feel like no one ever has and I want to feel this way for a very long time, in fact forever."

Kabir then pulled out a promise ring from his pocket and slid it into Kaamya's finger.

She was on cloud nine! Her someone special actually listened to her, knew her fears, and did everything in his power to make her feel special.

Kaamya said, "Kabir thank you so much for today and for making me feel so special it means a lot to me and I am sorry I got pissed at you, but I was just going through a lot and I just wanted your love and thank you so much for being patient and tolerant with me and making me smile when I wanted to cry."

In response to this Kabir just gave Kaamya a forehead kiss and that made her feel like home.

Kaamya thought "Isn't it amazing how someone we didn't even care about a few months ago now means the world to us."

Then she drove home and every song that she heard reminded her of Kabir!

She was smiling and laughing all day!

She wasn't high on drugs, she was high on love.

She would text Kabir all day and they would be on call at least for an hour and they were getting to know each other inside out.

Kabir knew so much about Kaamya that he could actually give competition to Raj who had known Kaamya all her life.

Kaamya on the other hand was just happy listening to Kabir because he didn't talk much but with Kaamya he would tell her everything, every single detail of his life and Kaamya loved getting to know Kabir.

16th August 2019

She was going to meet Kabir and she didn't know what it was but something felt different.

He texted her "wear something nice beautiful, can't wait to see you."

Now she went through all her clothes and finally settled on a black dress.

He told her to come to their spot so she went and when she reached she saw him smile at her cheekily so she asked, "what happened why are you smiling so much?"

So he went down on his knees, held the java chip in his hand and replied

"Kaamya since the day I met you every-day has been thrilling, I look forward to waking up every morning just to talk to you, I look forward to our walks in these lanes and I have realized that we are amazing together because no one can deny the chemistry that we have, we can solve every single problem when we are together, we make the best team, I would love to treat you like the queen you are, I love you Kaamya, I want to grow old with you, will you be my girlfriend?

First Kaamya took the java chip from his hand and said

"Finally you got the courage to ask me this question! Of course, I will be your girlfriend but on few conditions first, you will never leave and break my heart, second, we will always be us no matter what and third you will have to handle my drama.

He said "of course ill handle your drama it adds so much character to you, babe!'

The minute he said babe her happiness was on a different level.

She was in a relationship, a real relationship where they actually knew each other and they also loved each other truly.

The next few months passed by very quickly and as it is said when you spend time with the people you love time flies. When Kaamya was with Kabir hours would feel like seconds. She was living her life with him, but things between Raj and Riya had ended.

30th October 2019

Kaamya knew Kabir's exams were starting and he wouldn't be able to meet her so she wanted to make something special for him that would keep him motivated and tell him how much she loved him.

So she got a few of their pictures printed and made a collage out of it, then she wrote him few letters, she knew that she could call and text him but letters were always way more special.

Her letter said

"Dear Kabir,

I want you to know that you are the best thing that has happened to me. You have changed me so much for the better that to unknowingly. It was very obvious that we liked each other and us dating was inevitable. Our relationship literally feels like a dream! You know what's going on in my head just by looking at me and you always take me piggyback when my feet start hurting.

I will always have your back and no matter what happens you and I will never change! Finding love in this cruel world is very difficult but after I met you I know it's worth it! You make my life so much better just by being a part of it!

The time that I have spent with you is priceless and you mean the world to me. I know you're really worried about your exams but I know you will do really well! I love how you are so dedicated to what you want, and trust me all your hard work will pay off! I love you

Yours Kaamya"

Then she added a pen drive with their favourite music and added some chocolates and few vouchers to the local book store!

She then decorated the box and left to meet Kabir!

When Kabir saw the box he was shocked he had never expected Kaamya to take so much effort Kaamya told him to open the box at home, she gave him a hug and said "I believe in you, you will do great babe.", then Kabir gave Kaamya his sweatshirt and his perfume so that if she ever missed him she could just wear it and then she left.

Kabir went home and when he opened the box he was grateful to the universe for sending a beautiful soul like Kaamya's in his life!

Kabir and Kaamya had changed tremendously for each other Kabir who was usually very egoistic never let his ego come in the way of their relationship, and

Kaamya who believed in destiny wanted to make her own destiny with Kabir!

She always told Kabir "we are meant to be"

And Kabir believed in Kaamya and he had complete faith in their relationship.

A month passed by and Kaamya and Kabir had just been focusing on their careers. That was one thing both of them had in common, they were extremely career-oriented and so they never came in the way of each-others careers. Kaamya would wake Kabir up at five so that he could study and she would make sure she wasn't disturbing him!

For Kabir Kaamya was his stress releaser he would speak to her and get his energy back

Chapter 5

Kabir's exams were over and he had promised to give Kaamya all of his time so in the last five days they had gone on four dates and every time they went somewhere Kaamya would kick him from under the table, she would text him even if they were sitting in front of each other and she would tease him with his ex-girlfriend's name and she would never get insecure because she trusted him immensely.

Kabir really liked Kaamya's childish, happy go lucky nature, it made Kabir smile even in times of stress and it made him believe that everything would get better!

Both of them were complementary to each other that is, combining in such a way to enhance the qualities of each other. Kabir was extremely serious and Kaamya was carefree, Kabir was a person who loved luxuries and Kaamya found happiness in the small moments of life. Kabir wanted his life to be filled with success and Kaamya wanted her life to be filled with success and love, these qualities maintained a certain balance in their relationship and also made it interesting

Kaamya also said "if you are with someone who is exactly like you it would be more convenient but there would be no surprises, no learning, no new experiences! But with someone who is different every day is unpredictable, not always for the good but even when it's bad you learn and I think that is what matters. Life is out of control and as scary as that might sound that is what makes it exciting you don't know what each day has for you! Every twenty-four hours we get a fresh start, we can make the day count or we can waste it, the choice is ours. The more different people you meet the better and more unique experiences you can have!"

31st December 2019

It was the last day of 2019 and Kaamya and Raj had hosted a party, all their friends were there Kabir, Jenny, Naksh and even Sanket had come to the party just to see Kabir and Kaamya together and "approve" of their relationship and 15 other people were attending the party!

The party was amazing and everyone was having the time of their life! That is when Kaamya and Jenny got into a huge fight and Kaamya was holding her tears back, Kabir saw that and took her to a quitter, silent place and asked her what was wrong!

She told him that Jenny was being very rude to her, Jenny was getting jealous of Kaamya's friendship with her new friends Zara and Lavanya.

She also told Kaamya to choose between her and Kabir

Kaamya tried to explain to Jenny that Jenny meant the world to her and that no one would ever replace her, but she didn't like the way Jenny told her to choose between the two most important people of her life.

But Jenny was used to always being Kaamya's centre of attention and now she couldn't digest the fact that someone had taken her place, it was too much for her to take, because Kabir was not only her love but also her best friend.

Then Kabir and Kaamya saw Jenny leave and the tears from her eyes wouldn't stop.

So Kabir told her "Kaamya some people aren't worth your tears, if she truly loved you she would be happy in your happiness and she would never tell you to choose between two important people of your life. If you think your life would be better without me then I have no problem with leaving because all I want is for you to be happy. I promise that the day I start coming in the way of your dreams and goals I will leave myself but until then I want to have the time of my life without you, you look beautiful when you smile and if tears ever stream down your face they should be tears of happiness only! I want to make you so happy that there would be no room for sadness in your life anymore!"

Kaamya almost had tears in her eyes but this time happy ones. He was all she could ask for infact he was much better.

She was speechless but her tears had spoken a million words. Kabir knew she loved him truly and for him that was the best new~year's gift.

It was 11:57 and he played Kaamya's all~time favorite song "my heart will go on" and they danced to that song and as they swayed all her problems disappeared!

She was on top of the world and she even ignored Rajs calls, she didn't want that moment to end and they kept dancing till it was 12:30.

Then Kaamya went out and to her surprise, Jenny had come back, both of them then apologized to each other and gave each other a tight hug

After which Kabir, Kaamya, Raj, Jenny and Naksh went for a drive and they had a crazy time.

Kaamya had never felt so alive before and now she wasn't on a normal adventure this time the adventure was love, one wrong move and you are back to square one, but one correct move takes you 10 steps ahead, and trust is the biggest lifeline on this adventure.

Kaamya and Kabir had made memories for a lifetime they were together till 4 am and even though Kaamya never thought that a man would make her so happy, but she was just scared of one thing, till he made her happy it was fine but he shouldn't become her happiness!

Kaamya had always been independent in all aspects and that is why she wouldn't like being dependent on another person to make her day good or bad!

But even she knew that the more serious the relationship would be the more the dependency increases.

The next few months were beautiful.

Kaamya and Kabir got extremely serious about each other and soon it would be one year to their relationship but to Kaamya it felt like it was only yesterday that she had gotten to know Kabir as a person

That was the beauty of their relationship they spoke to each other like they knew each other for years but their relationship felt extremely fresh and it never got boring.

They always found ways to keep the spark going. They would travel together and even spend some time apart because "distance makes the heart gro fonder."

16th august 2020

A year had already passed by and today was the day that Kaamya and Kabir were going to meet each-others parents.

They were going to eat lunch with Kabir's parents and dinner with Kaamya's.

They were literally meting each-others parents. That is how serious they had got about each other and their relationship.

Kaamya was extremely nervous, she didn't know what to wear or how to act around them, whether she should voice her opinions or not or how they would take her blunt and honest nature!

So Kabir told her to just be herself, he didn't want to change her in front of anybody, he loved her the way she was

They were going to meet at the taj hotel and Kaamya wore a dress that was appropriate yet bold because even she wanted to make sure his parents knew exactly how she was.

During her entire way to the hotel she was just nervous and as she reached she could hear her heartbeat in her ears, that's how scared she was!

When Kabir's mom saw Kaamya she gave Kaamya the warmest smile. Kaamya touched her feet but aunty took her in for a hug and she then said, "Kabir told me you're beautiful but he didn't tell me that you were drop-dead gorgeous."

Kaamya said, "thank you aunty it means a lot to me!"

So Kabir's mom said, "Kabir you are very lucky to have such an amazing love, I am happy for you son."

Kabir replied "I know right mom, even I wonder how I got so lucky."

After spending more time with them Kaamya realized that she had been stressing out for no reason and that Kabir's parents were absolute sweethearts and they loved Kaamya, probably a little more than they loved Kabir.

Before Kaamya left Kabir's dad told her and Kabir "looking at you two is making my soul and my heart happy, I am very happy for both of you. Finding love is very hard but once you find it never let it go, the love that both of you have is real and rare!"

Those sentences always stuck with Kaamya.

In the evening it would be Kabir's turn to meet Kaamya.

He was nervous so he called Mehul and Jenny to ask about what he should wear and how he should speak.

So Jenny told Kabir that he should wear ripped jeans, chains and look like a gangster, at first Kabir was confused but Jenny convinced Kabir and got him to trust her completely.

So instead of wearing the suit that Kaamya had chosen for Kabir, he wore some ripped jeans with a real gangster like shirt.

Kaamya's parents were meeting Kabir at the Ritz Carlton hotel.

So when he reached, Kaamya couldn't believe her eyes! Her mouth was left open and she was shocked!

Then Kabir started speaking really weirdly because Jenny had told him that Kaamya's parents didn't like soft spoken men.

So Kabir was being extremely disrespectful and Kaamya just couldn't understand what was happening, Kaamya's parents kept giving her looks and her mom even texted her saying " I thought Kabir was well spken amd he came from a good family, right now he looks like he just got out of a huge fight, are you sure about him?

Kaamya wanted this to be perfect but the situation was the exact opposite of perfect.

The good thing for Kabir was that Mr Sinha had just got a call from his office; it was an emergency so Kaamya's parents left.

The minute they left Kaamya asked Kabir "what on earth are you wearing, why were you speaking like you just came from a street fight and where is the suit I chose for you?"

So Kabir replied saying "I thought your parents didn't like soft-spoken men and they like rough and bad men especially gangsters,"

Kaamya was very confused so she asked him "who told you this?"

So he said, "your best friend Jenny, she told me all this and she also chose my outfit."

Instead of being angry at Jenny Kaamya started laughing, she then told Kabir "the truth is that my parents absolutely hate gangsters or violent people, they love soft-spoken and well-mannered people, and you just got pranked by Jenny. My parents probably hate both of us right now, you for being a gangster and me for choosing you! I have no clue how I'm going to go home and if my parents disown me I'm coming to your house!"

Kabir couldn't believe it and after two minutes of silence Kabir and Kaamya started laughing hysterically.

Kabir couldn't believe it; he had just ruined his first meeting with Kaamya's parents and instead of trying to fix it the couple had turned it into a joke! But they definitely called Jenny and cursed a lot.

Few days after Kabir decided to fix it and so he went to Kaamya's house with roses for her mom and a tie for her dad, when Kabir explained the situation everybody was laughing and after spending the evening with Kaamya's family, Kabir was already calling Kaamya's mom "mom "and Aahna was calling Kabir "jiju" but Mr Sinha was still sir because as all of us know fathers are usually very protective.

Mr Sinha liked Kabir but he didn't want to tell Kaamya that so soon!

As for Aahna she had never seen her sister so happy so she was very excited and pleased with her sister's choice, Aahna also loved Kabir because he always got Aahna her favorite chocolate ice cream and he would also help Aahna irritate Kaamya!

Kaamya loved how her family had accepted Kabir and Kabir was happy that he could fix the temporary problems.

The next month Kaamya had spoken to Kabir's mom more than she had to Kabir and visa versa.

Usually, Indian parents did not really accept relationships but Kaamya and Kabir had understanding parents who were absolutely fine with relationships as long as the person their child had chosen was sensible and compatible with their child.

They just wanted to see Kaamya and Kabir happy.

Kaamya thought to herself, "im honestly lucky that I have parents who understand me because most of my friends who have strict parents end up going against their parents. It is usually said the ones who look the most innocent do the most, but even the children are not to blame because their parents have very unrealistic expectations in regards to their children! For once they should be a friend to their child and not just a parent. All of us just want few things in life one of them being the love of our parents and understanding. Parents make a lot of sacrifices for their children but when their children need them the most they let their ego come in the way."

But then Kaamya remembered that she didn't have time to think about all this she had to finish writing her application

Kaamya wanted to go to Yale.

She knew that meant going away from Kabir but it also meant going closer to her dreams, and her dreams meant a lot to her.

Chapter 6

Kabir and Kaamya's life was going perfectly well but "nothing lasts forever" so even these unforgettable times were soon going to come to an end, whether anyone liked it or not.

So in the midst of their perfect love story, things were going to take a turn.

22nd January 2021

This day was going to be etched in the love story of Kaamya and Kabir not as the beginning but as the end.

Yes Kabir and Kaamya were going to end and this time it wasn't a prank, it was happening for real.

Usually when anyone asked Kabir about what his favourite love story was

Kabir would reply by saying "the love story of Kaamya and Kabir that is my favourite."

Turns out his and our favourite love story was going to end.

Kaamya got an email from Yale!

It was her acceptance letter!

Kaamya Sinha had dreamt about Yale since the day she heard of it and her dreams were finally going to come true!

She now had to choose, this was an important decision to make.

She was in a crisis either the love of her life or the dreams she had seen since she was born.

So Kaamya met Kabir at their usual spot, she was extremely nervous she didn't know how Kabir would react, if he would be ok or not.

Kabir was so excited to see Kaamya and he waited for her with her usual drink.

Kabir as usual said, "hey beautiful, how are you?"

Kaamya said "hey, im fine."

Kabir instantly knew something was wrong so he asked her "what's wrong? Why do you sound so low is everything alright?"

Kaamya didn't know how to tell Kabir that in the next few minutes everything except their relationship was going to be fine.

So she told him everything "so Kabir actually I got accepted in Yale."

Kabir was thrilled to hear that he said "all your dreams are going to come true babe! Why are you so sad about it?"

So Kaamya said, "I am sad because if I choose my dreams it means that you and I are over."

That hadn't clicked Kabir's mind because he was too busy being happy for Kaamya.

They were both silent for few minutes, they didn't know what to say.

This was the first time Kaamya was meeting Kabir and she wasn't happy!

Kabir then said "Kaamya this is your dream don't give up on it! I know how much you wanted Yale, this is a big opportunity for you don't let it go!"

Kabir had just made Kaamya realize how much she loved her dreams.

Kaamya said, "Kabir will you be fine without me?"

So Kabir answered "no Kaamya I'll be miserable if you go, but if you don't go for me then I will die of guilt because the girl I love had to give up on her dreams because of me.

Kaamya had no words she just hugged Kabir one last time and said "I will never forget you."

Kabir then reminded her "if you remember I had told you that the day I start coming in the way of your dreams I will leave myself, Kaamya I love you, my happiness lies in your happiness, I don't know when I changed so much but my main motive in life isn't success anymore its just seeing a smile on your face and I know that nothing would make you smile more than Yale, I think its true 'you only know you love her when you let her go' I don't know how or when Ill be able to move on but I just want you to chase your dreams and believe in yourself."

Kaamya was in tears she said "Kabir I have no words to explain my love for you, I am so grateful to have you, if someone else was in your place they would be selfish and tell me to not chase my dreams but you inspire and motivate me every single day to achieve my goals, you have taught me how to put myself first and how to believe in myself. I am so glad that you were a part of my life and the times that I've spent with you have taught me a lot, I just want to tell you one more thing, I love you and I am grateful to you for being so selfless and understanding and I am sorry things are ending but in the end its all destiny."

She then said goodbye and left, and she didn't even turn around to wave or look at him one last time, that was Kaamya, for her it was always

DREAMS > LOVE

As she sat in her car the tears wouldn't stop streaming down her face, she just lost the one and only person she loved, to her dreams, but she knew her dreams were worth it.

Kabir, he is probably the most selfless person ever seen, not only did he sacrifice his love for her goals but he also inspired her and promised her that the day he would come in the way of her dreams and goals he would leave himself and indeed he did. He told the girl he loved to choose her career over him, any girl who had a man like him would be blessed and honestly Kaamya did lose out on something, now she felt like there was a hole in her heart.

With these thoughts on her mind she went home, her eyes were swollen because of crying and when she stepped out her family was playing hide and seek, but this time even they couldn't make her laugh.

When her mom saw Kaamya she was shocked so she went to Kaamya and asked her "what's wrong? What happened?"

This was probably the first time Kaamya was sad after she had met Kabir. Even her mom was shocked.

Kaamya then had a severe breakdown, she started crying and then she told her mom everything, her mom then took Kaamya to her room and knew that it would be best to give Kaamya her space, that night Kaamya cried herself to bed.

The next morning she woke up with a heaviness in her bones and she was breathing the hurt from her lungs, she hadn't realized it but Kabir had become her happiness and she was dependent on him. Her eyes looked hollow, drained, her face was pale.

Whether she accepted it or not Kaamya Sinha probably the world's most independent, bold girl was extremely dependent on someone else for her happiness.

Kaamya had never needed anyone in her life, she had been solo for the longest time because even she knew that the days she would fall in love she would fall hard and indeed she had fallen hard but there was no one to catch her, she didn't want anyone to catch her perhaps she wanted to feel the hurt, the pain, she wanted to see what its like to fall and then rise back up.

Life for Kaamya always meant thrill but after she met Kabir her heart had started beating for him, she never thought they would end, even when she dreamt of Kabir she always saw them grow old together,

The minute she closed her eyes she saw all the memories, the times that they had spent together flash infront of her eyes, she couldn't believe that this was the end for them, no more dancing on tables, no more going on dates, no more watching movies together or calling each other every night.

This was it Kaamya's love story had come to an end.

She just remembered how they had met and how they fell in love so unexpectedly, with Kabir everything was smooth and she never put a mask on her face when she met him, everything was real, the love, the thrill, the fun and even the pain.

Even though Kaamya was broken, even though her heart was shattered in a million pieces she still put herself together and went down, she had to be strong for herself, her friends and her family.

No matter how hard she tried the people close to her could see through those hollow eyes, she kept pretending it would be alright but deep down she had lost all her might. She changed the journey while reaching the destination but maybe the destination isn't worth the change, in the end when shes in the box her dreams won't be begging for her to return but the person who would do it would indeed be her love.

The next few days were very difficult for Kaamya. She felt scorched, apathetic and hollow, she kept reading depressing quotes and watched movies which had heartbreaks in them so that she would know she isn't alone.

One day she came across this paragraph and she connected to it so much that she wrote it in her journal. The paragraph said

"I left somebody who loved me despite my many, seemingly unforgivable fault. The words I spoke were daggers and my actions venom. Combined it was a brutal massacre of a loving heart. Pure and beautiful. Flawed perfection. This Earth holds many beauties, treasures beyond your wildest dreams. But nothing compares to him."

It was true. She knew there were plenty of other fish in the sea but she didn't want anyone else she just wanted Kabir.

She kept hoping that this feeling was temporary and she just wanted to get better everyone would constantly tell her to give it some time but sometimes time makes the wound grow bigger, what if Kaamya never recovered from this heartbreak? What if she never had the courage to love someone again?

She had broken Kabir and herself and the guilt was killing, Kaamya was very strong mentally so she didn't think about killing herself but isn't that what comes to the mind of most of us, when we think of our life without the people we love, it doesn't have to be your love or your soulmate, it could be your mother, you family, your friends or even yourself, because a lot of times to fit in we lose ourselves and the biggest battles that we fight are the wars between our mind and heart.

Every day she would wake up with a burden on her shoulders, she had been carrying that burden on her for so long that now it was weighing her down.

There were hardly any days left for Kaamya to leave for Yale but instead of being happy and thrilled she was sad and she didn't want to go.

Kaamya was spending all her time with her loved ones because they were her last few days in Pune, all of them would go for dinner or lunch.

2nd February 2021

It had been exactly eleven days to the break up and Kaamya was still miserable but she had learnt how to put on a fake mask on her face and smile even when she was crying on the inside.

She was going for dinner with her family and this time they picked a spot otherwise usually Kaamya would pick a spot. They asked Kaamya if she would be fine and Kaamya said yes but deep down she didn't know how she would react.

They first went to Café Coffee Day and when Kaamya saw that place she could see her and Kabir get her order and sit and talk about everything, then she saw them dancing on the tables, because she had visited that place so much the employees already knew Kaamya and her order and they even asked her "where is that man you usually come with?"

She didn't know how to respond so she just said "oh he is actually busy."

Everybody was used to seeing Kaamya with Kabir, even Kaamya couldn't see herself without him but she tried being strong.

As she drove through the lanes and the roads all she could see was herself with him.

When she was there she felt complete like she was never broken in the first place.

Kaamya had become numb, she had stopped feeling things, she started living by the quote "change is the only constant in life."

There were days when Kaamya would wake up to emptiness in her heart! Not only did she feel lonely but she also felt suffocated, like she couldn't breathe, like her heart wasn't beating, like the blood wasn't rushing through her head.

She felt numb, to be precise numb means to be deprived of feelings or responsiveness. When it comes to physical numbness a local anesthesia would probably work but for a broken heart only love could work.

7th February 2021

Kaamya was broken and as usual Sanket was taking care of her but this time it wasn't easy.

Raj, Mehul and Jenny also tried their best nut nothing worked, so they thought it was best to give kaamya time.

Chapter 7

Kaamya was in Yale! Yale was Kaamya's dream school. She had once heard of it and after doing her research Kaamya was breathing Yale every-day. Kaamya loved walking through the beautiful campus and she also participated in the Yale music festival. Kaamya had explored everything in Yale from the Yale Center for British Art, College Street Music Hall, City Hall, Cross Campus Library she'd eaten food at ivy noodle and pizza at York side pizza and she loved the Beinecke Rare Book and Manuscript Library.

Kaamya was a true wanderer and she loved traveling.

But still, sometimes she missed Kabir, even though she had gotten used to it, even though she had learned how to live life without him, she had accepted the fact that he wasn't coming back, but then on few days she would just wake up to the thought of Kabir, she would see memories play through her head, she got flashbacks of them together, having fun, running around the streets, acting like kids, dancing on tables and they were moments like these when Kaamya would realize that she had moved on but she couldn't get over him, yes there is a different move on means to go on to a different person place or subject and Kaamya had left Kabir and gone to Yale but getting over him means having no leftover residual of feelings, and that Kaamya couldn't do because she still loved Kabir and somewhere she always would.

A wise soul once said "sometimes you have to accept the fact that certain things will never go back to how they used to be"

Then after a point, Kaamya started writing her feelings down because she thought that writing them down would simplify her feelings.

For some of us the best way to deal with our problems is to run away from them but for Kaamya dealing with her problems meant confronting them.

Kaamya had always been like this bold, strong, and straight forward.

Kaamya usually preferred speaking but then she wrote a book and there was just one quote in that book which hit hard

It said

"Writing is like alchemy,

But instead of turning lead to gold,

 You change struggles to stories,

Such that others find solace in your strife,

As you turn words to warm hugs,

And anecdotes to affirmations

Of our beauty in imperfection."

Since the day Kaamya read this quote she started writing, she loved the idea of helping others by sharing her own problems this way even she would feel lighter and other people would realize that they aren't the only people going through that particular problem.

Kaamya had also made a lot of friends there Abhi, Kyra etc.

She was super close to Abhi and both of them would love hanging out with each other.

But deep down Abhi had started getting feelings for Kaamya and he really liked her.

Yes, this was going to be a mess.

Abhi and Kaamya had gone to the mall where they were choosing clothes for each other because they had a party to attend the next day.

Abhi got Kaamya a beautiful dress and Kaamya got Abhi a decent outfit.

Both of them then went back to the dorms and then the next day Kaamya got ready to go to the party

She was wearing a stunning black dress, it was backless, and Kaamya loved wearing bold clothes because she thought that her personality would shine through her clothing.

Abhi came and picked Kaamya up and the minute Kaamya entered the car Abhi's jaw dropped he had never seen a more beautiful woman, then Kaamya snapped at him and said "are you done staring at me? If you then start driving we're getting late!"

Abhi just looked around in embarrassment and started driving!

Then once they reached the party they saw that everyone was high or drunk, it was a usual college party, Kaamya loved parties and dance floors, if Kaamya was dancing there is no one else you would be able to look at anyone else.

Then she started dancing and Abhi was mesmerized by her eyes and the way she moved, he really liked Kaamya and he knew she was his best friend but he couldn't control his mind or heart, because in the end, everything is fair in love and war.

But things never end well when you fall in love with your best friend.

Hopefully, things would be different with Kaamya and Abhi.

In that party Kaamya was done dancing so she wanted to use the washroom, but she was too drunk to even walk, when she reached the washroom she forgot to lock the door and suddenly an extremely drunk guy walked in.

Kaamya tried to tell him to leave but he started pushing himself onto her, she was trying to push him away but she wasn't strong enough and the drinks were acting on her head.

That guy kept forcing himself onto her and she kept screaming, finally Abhi heard her and rushed to the washroom, then Abhi and the guy got into a huge fight. This was the first time Kaamya had seen Abhi get into a fight, usually he would keep calm and maintain peace. Kaamya was shocked but too scared to say anything so she just let Abhi drop her back to her dorm.

The next morning was extremely weird, Kaamya had a hangover but she still remembered the events that had occurred that night.

She kept hoping that it was just a bad dream but it wasn't, it was the sad reality.

Then Abhi came over with some chocolates to help Kaamya feel better, but she just kept imagining what could have happened if Abhi hadn't come and she hadn even gotten the chance to thank Abhi properly.

So she said, "Abhi thank you so much for always being there for me and supporting me, I literally don't know what I would do without you, the way you always have my back is incredible thank you so much for being such an amazing best friend."

Kaamya's words meant a lot to Abhi but he didn't want to just be her best friend he wanted to take this friendship forward, but he didn't know if Kaamya felt the same way about Abhi, but he knew that she was worth the risk, in the end all he wanted was Kaamya.

But Kaamya had no clue that her best friend likes her because Sanket and Kaamya had been only friends for the longest time.

But all fingers aren't the same similarly all people aren't the same, everyone is different.

Abhi was now planning a proposal for Kaamya and he wanted it to be perfect so he took Kaamya to a theatre and then after they finished watching the play, all the actors suddenly made a circle around Kaamya and sang 'something just like this' by chain-smokers. Kaamya was shocked but then she saw Abhi go down on his knees and say "Kaamya be my girlfriend"

Kaamya was shocked, she loved Abhi but just as a friend and she didn't know how he would react to a rejection and she just wanted to be best of friends with Abhi because she loved Abhi just not in that way.

So she subtly took Abhi to a side and told him "Abhi im sorry but I can't be your girlfriend, I love you but not in that way, you have been an amazing best friend but I don't think of you to be anyone more than that. I hope that this doesn't change our friendship but I don't think I would do justice to me or you if I lied about my feelings. I apologies once more but please don't change and stay the same."

Abhi was heartbroken, he thought he had found the love of his life but deep down even he knew that Kaamya was Kabir's and she would never give her heart to anyone else!

Kaamya still slept wearing Kabir's sweatshirt and she still reread all their old conversations, she would call him just to hear his voice, she still felt her heartbeat rise when someone said his name, she would feel like her life would stop if she ever saw him again but life has its ways of bringing people back to the track.

While Kaamya was studying in Yale chasing her dreams, Kabir had changed everything about him, his appearance etc, and he would just run away from his feelings, he didn't know how to deal with heartbreak, he didn't know how to live without Kaamya so instead of thinking about it he kept himself extremely busy, he would keep working or studying.

Kabir had cut all contact with everyone who was related to Kaamya except her mother. Kabir still spoke to Kaamya's mom to make sure Kaamya is fine and for him Kaamya's mom was actually his mom so he loved speaking to her. She also reminded Kabir of Kaamya but everyone was extremely proud of Kabir for letting Kaamya go, very few people can let go of their love.

Kabir and Kaamya were like parallel lines perfect for each other but they never met.

Kabir was helping his dad with the business and when his parents would ask him about Kaamya he would just change the topic, Kabir's parents knew that he was just putting a hard front but he was really hurt on the inside, so one day he left a voicemail to Kaamya and he spoke to her like she was a stranger.

He said "I think its so messed up how we can go from talking to a person day and night, for hours and hours, creating memories with them, going on dates, walks, watching movies together, losing sleep because we're talking all night, having them wipe your tears when we're upset. We were so happy but then suddenly, one day, everything changed, when the person that we love more than our self leaves we are broken and no matter how much people try to fix it we don't let anyone in, we feel like everyone who comes will leave and we push everyone away just to protect ourselves, but protecting yourself isn't a choice, everyone needs to do it, love is not made for the weak hearted. Life teaches us a lot, people teach us a lot and Kaamya you taught me how to put myself first, now I know why you told me to love myself. I hope you are fine and I know this was abrupt but it has been on my mind for a very long time now and I just wanted to say it."

When Kaamya heard this voice mail she was in tears. It was probably the first time in years that Kaamya had heard Kabir's voice.

She didn't know how to react, she felt like she had broken him, his voice had always been Kaamya's weakness, but this time his words had hit hard,

Kaamya broke down terribly so she called Aarya.

Aarya was Kaamya's cousins both of them weren't close at first but then one day there was an emergency and Aarya had come to Kaamya's house, that night both of them spoke for hours, they didn't even sleep and since that day both of them became best of friends. The minute anything important happens, both of them call each other, they were like each-others human diary, both of them knew each and every detail about each other, big or small.

Aarya was a blessing for Kaamya, when things had started to go south with Kabir Aarya was Kaamya's backbone. She would cover for Kaamya, listen to her talk all day and the best part was when she spent time reading zodiac posts on instagram all night. They didn't really believe in astrology but both of them liked the concept of blaming the occurrence of bad things on the moon.

So Kaamya was on a video call with Aarya all night and then she fell asleep.

The next morning Kaamya decided to forget about Kabir once and for all, so she started keeping herself extremely busy and she would avoid talking about Kabir.

As you all know by now for Kaamya nothing was more important than her dreams.

Kaamya had moved on with her life, of course she couldn't forget Kabir but she wasn't bothered by looking at people or things anymore.

Few days later Kaamya was speaking to her mom.

Her mom kept bringing up her childhood memories and Kaamya was missing home.

She missed her mom, dad, Aahna, grandmom and grandad.

The times that she had spent with her family were irreplaceable and unforgettable.

She missed all the fun, the music, the dance, the festivals and the togetherness.

Her mom then reminded her of an incident that had taken place when Kaamya was in ninth grade. So Kaamya wanted to go to meet her friends and then stay over at one of her friend's house but her mom didn't allow her to step out of the house.

Kaamya being Kaamya wanted her thrill and adventure even at that time so she jumped from the window of the first floor and then she sneaked out, Kaamya called her friends and they all went for a drive. They sang songs, put their head out of the window and even got chased by the cops.

Then when Kaamya was at her door she realized that she had left her keys inside. She didn't know what to do, jumping down the first floor was easy but actually climbing back up was going to be a task, so Kaamya tried to climb up and when she had almost reached, her leg slipped and she fell.

That says Kaamya got a fracture and she couldn't walk straight for months. Her mom just said one thing "next time when I say something earn to listen."

At that time it wasn't serious but both of them had laughed a lot later.

Chapter 8

Kaamya was on her plane to Pune, she was going back permanently after five years and her family had never been more excited!

Her house was extremely chaotic just like her mind, she didn't know how she felt about going back to India after all these years, but of course, she was happy to be back home.

As for everyone in the house, they were all doing special things for Kaamya.

Her grandmother was making Kaamya's favorite food, her grandfather was singing a song for her, her mom had gone shopping to get her favorite clothes, her dad was learning how to dance, her sister had made a frame of all their pictures and redecorated her room and the neighbors had made her a cake!

It was perfect, that was Kaamya, everyones favorite, it was really hard to hate her, she was good at almost everything and she had her whole life planned.

She didn't give anyone a chance to complain, with her everything was correct and so he made sure everyone was happy.

If anyone was upset the first person that they would go to would be Kaamya, she had the solution for everything and she made everyone feel warm and safe.

So as Kaamya reached the airport she saw her parents there.

They had come to pick her up and take her home, on her way home she was telling everybody about her life and how it had changed Kaamya.

Kaamya hadn't changed much, but the experiences had made her wiser.

When they reached home she was so happy to be back.

All the chaos had died down both in her mind and in the house

When she saw her house all the confusion was over, she knew that no matter where she went she would always come back home.

The next few weeks Kaamya didn't do much, she met up with old friends, spent a lot of time with her family and shopped a lot.

She also met Aarya and went to phoenix.

Over there both of them shopped so much that their pockets were empty and they had spoken about the whole world.

They then planned a sleepover and just like old times they spent the entire night reading zodiac signs and posts, somethings never change and they were best left untouched.

Kaamya then also watched videos of weddings, family functions and festivals to see what she had missed out on.

She cracked up when she saw her cousins dancing! They still couldn't dance at all and the way they were copying each other was adorable.

One of these days Kaamya also visited her old house and there she met all her childhood friends and the people that she had grown up with.

Life in those times was so easy, Kaamya didn't have to think about anything. Her biggest problems were scars on her knees and fights between her dolls.

Life changes so much so soon, one day we're playing with dolls and the other day we're playing with our lives.

It feels like time just passes by and we lose out on memories.

Life is colourful but without love, everyone's life is black and white!

In Kaamya's life she had only loved once and it was probably the best experience of her life!

She always said, "I don't regret falling in love it was one of the best decisions I made, I'm not sad its over I am happy it happened."

The next day Kaamya was going to Café Coffee Day to meet a friend.

When she reached she saw that her friends hadn't reached yet so she placed her order and texted her, then she replied saying a family emergency had come up so she wouldn't be able to make it and then she apologised.

Since Kaamya had already reached the location and placed an order she thought that it would be nice if she just spent some time alone, the last few days had been extremely hectic for her and she had hardly given herself time.

As she sat in the café she remembered all the times she had met Kabir there, all those memories made her realize that she still loved him but it was pointless.

Just when she was looking around she saw Kabir! Kaamya couldn't believe her eyes, she thought she was just imagining things as usual but then he saw her and came to her table.

He asked her politely "is this seat taken?"

Kaamya stammered at first not knowing how to react and then said "um, no"

So he sat down and then realized that she was drinking the same coffee that she always ordered. She used to order the same coffee even five years back.

He looked at the coffee, chuckled and then said "some things never change."

Kaamya was confused, she didn't know what Kabir was referring to.

Kabir understood by the look on her face and explained "im talking about the coffee."

Kaamya blushed, she liked how Kabir had observed that she still ordered the same drink and she was shocked that he even remembered her order.

So Kaamya asked, "what do you do now?"

Kabir replied saying "I've finally started my own business and it's doing pretty well!"

Kabir couldn't contain his curiosity and he asked "so are you single?"

Kaamya just laughed and said, "of course I am, no one could handle my obsession with my dreams, but I realized that love is more important than my dreams because success only tastes sweet when you have someone to share it with."

Kabir laughed and said "you still haven't changed at all! You still talk like a philosopher, if only you could think like this five years back."

Kaamya's face fell as she remembered the incidents that had taken place a few years ago.

Kabir realized and quickly changed the topic, he didn't want to make this meet up a sad one.

Soon both of them started discussing their past and the memories that they had made together. Life had a weird way of giving you what you need at the right time.

Later that day Kabir dropped Kaamya home, they had already made plans for the next few days.

Kaamya hadn't felt this anxious since the last time she was going to meet Kabir.

Kabir had an effect on Kaamya that no one else had and even after five years nothing had changed. They still had amazing chemistry and both of them were made for each other!

When Kaamya told her mom about her accidental meet up with Kabir her mom was so happy that she started dancing around.

She was happy that her daughter had found the love that she deserved again, her mom knew that Kabir was the one for Kaamya since day one and that's why she had always considered Kabir a part of the family.

The next few days Kaamya spent most of her time with Kabir, a lot of the times they would redo the things they did few years ago just in honour of the past.

But this time Kaamya realized that Kabir had changed, he had built a wall around himself and caged his heart.

After Kaamya had left it had been very difficult for Kabir to move on and start living his life without her, so after that day Kabir had become extra cautious with his heart.

He did still love Kaamya but he knew that if she left again the damage would be irreversible and he wouldn't be able to take it so he wanted to be sure that this time Kaamya's top priority was Kabir.

Kaamya wanted to make sure Kabir knew that he had nothing to worry about so she planned a surprise for him.

Kaamya took the help of her family members and planned a treasure hunt for Kabir. Each family member including Kabir's family was holding the hint and the last prize would be with Kaamya.

So Kaamya called Kabir home and the game began after Kabir found every clue he would get a note which said something like "I care about you" or "you mean a lot to me"

When Kabir finally reached Kaamya she was standing with a huge cardboard with all their recent pictures and then she flipped the board and It said "I will never leave or break your heart!" in bold!

That meant a lot to Kabir; he loved how she could still see through his eyes and tell when something is wrong.

Kaamya was glad that Kabir would probably finally let his guard down.

Everything was going well, but all of us know by now that if we feel like something is too good to be true then it probably is too good to be true.

Few days later Kaamya got a call from the hospital, the doctors said that Jenny had gotten into an accident and was admitted in the hospital, they said that Kaamya was the first person on speed dial.

Kaamya and Kabir rushed to the hospital and also informed Jenny's parents and Naksh!

Naksh and Jenny were still together, their bond and love was unbreakable.

As Kaamya saw Jenny tears rolled down her cheeks. Jenny was one person who had always stuck with Kaamya through the good and the bad. Jenny's situation was constantly getting worse and she had a chance of not surviving because the accident had damaged her head!

Kaamya didn't know what to do, she wanted to be strong but at the same time, she couldn't even bare the thought of losing her best friend.

Naksh was constantly crying, he couldn't keep his spirits up.

For the last five years, there were many times when Naksh wanted to give up but he didn't because he knew Jenny couldn't live without him and now seeing Jenny in this condition Naksh didn't have a reason to not give up.

Nobody was eating or sleeping, everybody was just extremely restless, the minute anyone even slept for a second they would get a nightmare.

Things weren't getting any better, Jenny wasn't responding at all, everyone had lost hope when suddenly one day Naksh went inside.

Naksh went inside and held Jenny's hand, he was controlling his tears and then he said "you can't leave me like this! What will I do without you?"

Jenny had started responding, not a lot but it was a start.

After that Kaamya and Naksh would take turns and meet Jenny and tell her about everything.

These small things were slowly making Jenny's condition better and the doctors said that it wasn't long till she would finally open her eyes!

Everyone had finally smiled in months.

One day when Kaamya was talking to Jenny, Jenny opened her eyes! Kaamya could not believe it; she called everyone Naksh, Kabir, her parents and the doctors!

Jenny had opened her eyes after months.

She just looked at Naksh and her parents and smiled.

Once she was in the state to move a bit she gave Kaamya a long hug.

Kaamya and Kabir would visit Jenny every-day and they would make sure she didn't get depressed in that hospital room!

Jenny was recovering fast and soon she was discharged.

Naksh had decorated Jenny's room and he had also called all her friends so that she felt livelier.

When Jenny entered her room she literally had tears in her eyes.

This incident had opened every-one's eyes.

They had all understood that life is unpredictable and that we shouldn't take anyone for granted!

These thoughts had completely taken over Kabir's mind and Kabir had been getting nightmares ever since.

Kabir was getting nightmares of losing Kaamya and Kabir could not take that risk again so Kabir knew that it was time for him to make some life changing decisions.

Kabir planned for months and then one fine day he was ready for the execution.

Kabir called Kaamya and told her to meet him at their spot, which was obviously the lane.

When Kaamya reached the beginning of the lane she saw Jenny who took Kaamya forward.

When Kaamya looked at the street she was shocked. There were rose petals along the footpaths, lights hanging up and the road was lit up beautifully.

Then Jenny randomly went in front and started dancing to music, soon Naksh joined her. Then

Kaamya moved forward and she saw Riya and Reshma aunty dancing to their favourite song.

Kaamya kept moving and as she moved she saw Aarya, Raj, Aahna, her grandparents and even Sanket perform! Kaamya was shocked when she saw Sanket there.

The second last performance was Kaamya's parent and then she saw Kabir.

He was wearing a black suit with a tie. By the time he walked in Kaamya already had tears in her eyes! The most important people of her life had dedicated dances and speeches to her!

Even Sanket had come to Pune just for two hours.

When Kabir entered everybody went silent. First, he performed and danced and then he said

"Kaamya you are the most beautiful, smart, pretty and amazing women that I know. When I met you few years ago I didn't know you would mean so much to me! I didn't know that you'd mean anything to me but now you are my world! When I spend time with you I become happier, you make me a better person altogether, you bring out the best in me at all times and life without you is dull and boring. Only I know how I've survived these years without you because trust me there have been times I didn't want to live but the only thing that kept me alive in our memories! This may sound very cliché but life without you is no life at all. I may be living but im not alive without you. Even when you left I was yours and even when you're here I'm yours. When Jenny was in that hospital and she had almost lost her life, I realized that life is uncertain. Today we're alive but tomorrow we might be dead and I don't want to live even a second without you, Kaamya you might be all about the thrill and you are probably very different than me but I want you to know that if you and me we are together than we can do anything."

He then looked at Kaamya's parents and said "sir, maam, do I have your permission to ask for your daughters hand in marriage?"

Both the parents said yes!

Then Kabir went down on his knees, opened his ring box, and said "Kaamya you are the love of my life and I want to wake up every morning next to you, I love you. We are meant to be. Will you marry me?"

Kaamya was in tears, she couldn't ask for more all she did was nod and then Kabir slid the ring in her finger.

Both of them hugged each other and then the families celebrated.

Kaamya was probably the happiest human alive that day.

That night when she lay in her bed she just thought about her journey with Kabir. It had been a rollercoaster.

She remembered how five years back she had told Kabir that they weren't meant to be, and now they were soon going to get married.

That is why it is said "what is yours will come to you" and "if you're meant to be you will be."

Kabir and Kaamya were meant for each other and that's why even after they separated ways their paths met again.

No matter what you do in life your destiny always has a way of giving what you deserve. In Kaamya's case it was Kabir, in your case it might be different.

Remember one thing "live each day like it's your last day and a make decisions like you are never going to die."